Aloha Kiki

Ten Tips to a Better You

Sofia Kehaulani Selbe

ISBN 978-1-0980-3456-6 (paperback)
ISBN 978-1-0980-3457-3 (digital)

Christian Faith Publishing, Inc.
832 Park Avenue
Meadville, PA 16335
www.christianfaithpublishing.com

Printed in the United States of America

Contents

Introduction

Dear friend, this book is a gift from me to you. Through the words I am writing to you, I hope you will gain new enzymes in your body to create a healthier life for yourself. These pages are full of antibodies against the worst of things life has. Each passage will be a new candle lighting your way down the path to a more positive lifestyle. May your body be strengthened from the inside out, and may your mind be trained to handle things in a new way. This book was created from the pieces of my heart and designed by the thread of my mind.

The inspiration to write this book comes from our Instagram page @alohakiki808 and the wonderful fans who have encouraged us to move forward in printing our daily messages from our Instagram into a physical book to carry around in times you are not online. This book should be used as a guide to create the best version of yourself with our very simple tips.

We wanted to break down the book into segments that were simple enough to precisely pinpoint areas of your life that will be positively impacted with our words.

The contents are a collection of the captions of posts from our Instagram, and now they are even more in-depth and organized for you to fully understand.

Dear friend, we appreciate your support, and we send you off on this bright self-discovery quest with the warmest aloha.

Enjoy your *Daily Dose of Aloha Kiki*.

Chapter 1
You Are...

Never let anyone treat you like regular glue. You *are* glitter glue. You deserve to be treated in *high* standards. Do not allow others to downgrade you. It is important to expect respect from everyone you encounter. By respecting yourself, you are showing others how to treat you. Enforce your values for yourself. Do not fall for the inadequacy of the standards placed by inadequate people. The right people will respect you, and those who do not should not be in your life. Stop falling for the negativity of this world and start standing for the positivity.

You *are* fearfully and wonderfully made. Each of us is designed with great intentions. We each have talents and traits that create our identities. No two souls are the same. We are all precious masterpieces. Embrace your uniqueness, never change who you are, and define what sets your soul on fire.

You *are* enough. Today and every day, remember that you owe it to yourself for having the strength to carry on. Yes, sometimes we all fall short of our own expectations, and we push ourselves over the edge in order to fulfill them. But not anymore! Remember how much you matter, and you are enough.

You *are* a diamond; you did well under pressure. A diamond is formed in the earth's mantle with immense heat and compression. We all are diamonds being formed in our lives' mantles with immense challenges and struggles. We all are ignited and pushed through situations we never prepared for, but these situations make us stronger and wiser for the future. Remember, you are a diamond, precious and strong. Life cannot break you.

Chapter 2
You Are Not...

You are *not* meant to be at the bottom of your to-do list. Put yourself at the top of your to-do list today and watch everything else fall into place. We all need to take a step back and take a look at how we are treating ourselves. Sometimes we have to make ourselves the priority, and we should not feel bad about that. You are absolutely important and never a waste of time.

You are *not* lucky, just blessed. Remember how blessed you are every day, and delight in your life's greatest blessings. Every day we can find a blessing that will allow us to move past any worries we may have. There will always be at least one thing we can be blessed by. It could very well be a person, and it very much so could be your trusty pup. Look deep into your little blessing's eyes, and know that you are "not lucky, just blessed."

You are *not* a product of your failures. Failure built more heroes than privilege ever could. If you never fail, you never learn. A failure is a reminder that you are forgetting something. You are *not* being your best. If you fail, never give up because FAIL means *first attempt in learning*. Denis Waitley said, "Failure should be our teacher, not our undertaker. Failure is a delay, not defeat. It is a temporary detour, not a dead end."

You are *not* what you have done, you are what you have overcome. Through all of life's turmoils, we must be able to overcome. We cannot allow our battles to leave us beaten. We can rise back up, and we can do better. These challenges that life gives us are all important lessons. Yes, we have done things that do not always turn out the way we planned, we have done wrong, and we have done bad. But we are not what we have done; we are what we have overcome. Leave behind the hurting and lean toward the healing.

Chapter 3
You Should...

You *should* become so confident in who you are that no one's opinion, rejection, or behavior can rock you. You *should* be authentically yourself. Muscle up your courage and get over your fears that others have control over you. Unlock your heart, and overflow with kindness.

The only time you *should* look back is to see how far you've come. We all go through some very difficult and stressful things. We think we will never get through it. We feel trapped. We feel forgotten. We feel like there is no way we can move forward. *But* no matter how incredibly hard it may seem at the time, we *will* be able to move forward. One day we will look back and see that we did it. We've come so far. Wow!

Be forever in love with creating the best version of yourself. Each day you *should* be zooming in and putting yourself under the magnifying glass. Create the best version of yourself by taking a closer look into those areas of yourself that need improvement. We should always want to do better and design a way of life that is fulfilling.

A girl should be like a butterfly—pretty to see but hard to catch. You *should* always give a little mystery behind yourself and you need not reveal so much to everyone.

You *should* only make decisions based on fabulousness. If it doesn't make you feel fabulous, don't do it, don't buy it, don't wear it, don't eat it, and don't keep it. In life, we all need to learn to ask ourselves, "Does this make me feel fabulous?" Because if you are in a bad relationship, hard job, family tragedy, or inner battle, you must assess your decisions. What *can* you do that *will* make you feel fabulous that you will be healed, uplifted, safe, peaceful, and healthy? Never do smothering that will hinder your well-being or create a worse situation than you are already in. Only do things that will give you a fabulous outcome.

Chapter 4

You Should Not...

I wonder how much of what weighs me down is not mine to carry.

You should *not* feel obligated to carry anyone else's baggage. You should *not* include yourselves with those who want to add their burdens to your load. Unload yourself of relationships that are toxic. Remove yourself from situations that keep you trapped. Embrace new experiences that can produce a lighter load in life.

You should *not* settle; you should strive. *Kūlia i ka nu'u*. Strive for the highest.

Kūlia i ka nu'u (pronounced ku-lee-ah-ee-kah-nooh-ooh) is the Hawaiian value of accomplishment and achievement. The literal translation for *Kūlia i ka nu'u* is "Strive to reach the summit." In life, there is always a mountain in front of you, and it is your best pursuit to climb to the top of that mountain and declare your destiny. Anyone who has this value of *Kūlia i ka nu'u* will continually pursue self-improvement and personal excellence. If you believe in this, you will consider your life and everything within it to be a "work in progress," and you will enjoy the effort. Hard work is good work when it employs the energy of striving and reaching higher.

You should *not* let anyone rent space in your head unless they are good tenants. You should *not* allow the small-minded opinionators to deprive you of large-minded dreams. You should *not* give them room to spread their misery. Mermaids don't lose sleep over the opinions of shrimp. You should *not* lose sleep from the screams of hatred and lies from the bad tenants of your mind. Kick them out; find new uplifting people to occupy your mind.

You should *not* compare yourself to others. Start watering your own grass. Invest in things that are special to you. Understand that you are a constant work in progress.

Chapter 5

You Can...

Ralph Marson said, "What you do today can improve all your tomorrows."

Oprah Winfrey also stated, "The biggest adventure you can take is to live the life of your dreams."

You *can* create the foundation of your dreams for the future, and you *can* live the life of your dreams now. Each day we have the power to improve our future. The actions we take and the choices we make will always do something to move us either forward or backward in our journey. What will you do today to improve your tomorrows? How many of you are still in high school or college and are working hard toward graduation? Are you doing little moves each day to get you closer to the finish line? Or are you in a beginner position and work and you want to climb the ladder? Are you proving to your supervisors that you are worthy of that promotion? Wherever you are, be sure to take a little time to plan for the next step ahead.

You *can* improve your current situation while still staying put. "We need not look outside our borders," said Prince Charming (*Cinderella*, 2015). Do what you *can* with what you have wherever you are. Your tools to designing a better life are right before you. Many times, we wish we could just teleport somewhere else, and all our problems would disappear. However, take a good look around right where you are, and you will be amazed at all the potential there is right where you are. It is not always about what we wish we could have; it is about using what we do have to fulfill our wishes.

You *can* lead others out of the dark. Remember those days that you felt stuck too.

Take a lamp of comfort and hold it out for others who are finding their way out of the darkness. Your spirit should sparkle and shine enough not only to illuminate all the wonderful things in your life but also to diminish all of the worrisome things in your life.

Chapter 6
You Can Not...

When something goes wrong, yell, "Plot twist!" and move on.

You can *not* control everything or everyone. Sometimes we have to turn the page, even if the cast from the previous chapter will not be in this new chapter. The story must go on without them. Many times, we think that we have it all figured out that nothing could go wrong. We come to the idea to show mercy to those who have hurt us in the past and to give them another chance. We let our hearts pour out forgiveness because we think we can solve everything. We planned that by giving this generous reconciliation with the thought that any brokenness can be mended. But then it totally goes wrong, and the trust we gave was thrust away. It is easy to blame ourselves for not planning better. How could we not foresee this happening? It was our fault from the moment we created this plot. But no, my friends, we should never blame ourselves for the wrongdoing of others. From now on we will know better. Yell, "Plot twist!" and get the heck away from those who throw mud at your mercy. You are worthwhile and meaningful, and they do not deserve to be in your story.

When you can *not* find the sunshine, be the sunshine. Some days you can *not* seem to get a break. Where is the sunshine when the entire world is dark and gloomy? The rain keeps pouring, and the wind keeps blowing. The sunshine has to come from inside of you. The outside will not change, then you will have to change. The quality of your life comes from the quality of your thoughts. Break the storm with the sunshine within you.

You can *not* influence the world by being just like it. No one is you, and that is your superpower. Take this superpower and use it to be an incredible influence in the world.

Chapter 7
You Will...

Cheers to no more fears! You *will* be fearless and confident in everything today.

Fearlessness is not the absence of fear; rather, it's the mastery of fear. Fearlessness means you are aware of the fear in your life, yet you press on despite the fear. You *will* get through the scary situations, you *will* move past the heartache, and you *will* master the fear creeping into your life. Try to balance the fear with faith. If you have faith that the fear will disappear, then you can push forward much easier. Every day you wake up with a bundle of blessings. You *will* have so many good things to be thankful for. You will never want to take one day for granted. Celebrate today. Why wait? Make today amazing. You are amazing. Life is amazing. Do not forget how great everything is. Once this day is gone, you will not have it again. So let us celebrate. Until further notice, celebrate everything. Cheers to no more fears!

One of the most important decisions you *will* ever make is to be in a good mood.

How hard is it to just be in a good mood? Some days it can feel extremely hard. Take care of your thoughts when you are alone, and take care of your words when you are with others.

Two things to always keep in check: one, your thoughts; and two, your words. Your mind can play tricks and create traps that make you feel less than your best. Your words can dispel harm and convey disrespect that make others feel less than their best. Always think before you speak to others, and always speak to others if what you are thinking is causing self-harm. Speak and think with love at the center.

If you light a lamp for someone else, you *will* also brighten your path. It is another bright day to show random acts of kindness to anyone around you. Even the smallest things can make the biggest impact. Go out and seek a way to light a lamp for someone new.

Chapter 8
You Will Not...

When someone says you can't do it, do it twice, and take pictures.

There will always be people wanting to bring you down, but you will *not* let them. Be strong, and fight for what you believe.

You will *not* be right all of the time, so be humble enough to accept constructive criticism. Constructive criticism is the process of offering valid and well-reasoned opinions about the work of others, usually involving both positive and negative comments, in a friendly manner rather than an oppositional one. We all need to reach out to friends, family, community leaders, teachers, and mentors to give us the tough love. If they love you, they will tell you about the booger in your nose, and you will take care of that booger before presenting yourself to strangers. First impressions mean a lot, so practice improvement with those who know you best first. You will *not* be the best version of yourself without making important changes. If done well, constructive criticism will not be awkward at all.

Be stubborn about your goals. Be flexible about your methods. You will *not* get to your goals without staying firm in your beliefs, but at the same time explore the many different methods you can use to reach this goal. Always be open to trying something new and exciting.

Happiness is not trying or finding—it's deciding. You will *not* have only days full of rainbows and butterflies; some days will be full of mud and wasps. You must decide for yourself how to deal with your situation in the best possible way.

Chapter 9

You Have...

HOPE—Have Only Positive Expectations.

You *have* so much to look forward to when you *have* hope. Be hopeful in each stage of your life. Hope that the best will happen. Maybe it won't happen immediately, but it will inevitably. When you expect a positive outcome, then your mind is retrained to grasp the struggles along the way. Always have *hope*.

You *have* more with gratitude in your heart. Gratitude enables our hearts to tell a better story. Gratitude is often taken for granted. Look around and see how much you really have. Be grateful for everything. There will always be someone who has much less than what you have. The best thing about today is that you are alive to experience it. You are given each moment, and it is your mission to make each moment your best moment yet. Accept what is, let go of what was, and have faith in what will be. The future before us is full of possibilities. We all need to accept what is happening now, let go of what was happening then, and have faith in what will be happening soon!

You *have* so many wonderful people in your life. Realize that near or far, there are many people who care about you. A fun saying is, "I wish that you were here or that I was there or that we were together anywhere!" Isn't the best place to be is wherever your closest friends and family are? Life is enriching when we are together. Together is such a precious word, and I feel instantly uplifted when I say it. Can you ever feel down when you say, "Let's do that together" or "Together we can" or "It doesn't matter as long as we are together"? All of these statements are inclusionary and instantly uplifting. We may not have it all together, but together we have it all.

You *have* the gifts of immeasurable talents. Use them all up before you leave this earth.

Chapter 10
You Have Not...

You have *not* come this far to only come this far. The greatest reward is not the achievement of the goal itself, but it is who you become along the way. The journey can be even better than the destination. You have *not* gone through this journey only to stop at the "final destination." The thing is, there is no final destination. Life will always have new journey ahead. The best thing about life is just when you think you are done, life gives you another challenge. To be completely done in life means you are dead. When you complete one goal, plan to complete the next one even better. Dream an even bigger dream. Take an even bigger risk. You have *not* stopped seeking, wondering, or contemplating. You have *not* stopped being curious. Along with each of our journeys, there are great pit stops. When we pause and soak up all the valuable lessons, we can push forward with even more strength. You have been assigned this mountain to prove it can be moved. Then once you have, find your next mountain.

You have *not* wasted time; you have only forgotten to put it where it mattered most. Time is one thing we cannot get back. Once time is spent, there arc no refunds. However, we can spend it wisely if we allocate time to what truly matters in our lives. Portion a time-out each day for those you love. If you use love as the deciding variable for where time is spent, then you will see a better return for your investment. You have *not* invested so much of your time to feel guilt, anxiety, worthlessness, or abandonment. Create a timetable with a hierarchy each day and put time into the best things for your life. It hurts when you think you have wasted your time. You feel the sting of regret, and the only remedy is a change in perspective. Instead, say, "I have *not* wasted my time. I have only forgotten to put it where it mattered most."

Final Thoughts

I started writing this book over a year ago, and I would have never thought that Kiki Sunshine would not be here with me when the book was finally published. Kiki's given name from her birth was Sunshine, and she truly lived up to that name for her soul was the brightest of them all. She had the most radiant smile, warm and compassionate. Kiki Sunshine was the healthiest and happiest pup, without one bad day in her life. She was only nine years young, and in January I eagerly bought all the supplies for her tenth birthday coming up on August 28. Everything in the early parts of this year was going so well. We had so many fun things planned to do. However, out of the blue, on what seemed like another normal day turned into the most tragic day. A silent killer, also known as a blood clot, lodged itself right next to Kiki's heart. Blood clots can happen to anyone, even super healthy people or pets. No one would have known she had it. She could have just died without anyone around. But by God's mercy, I was right with Kiki from the moment this all started. I knew something was wrong because Kiki couldn't breathe. She was coughing hard and went to lay down next to the front door. Thank God I acted swiftly and got Kiki immediately to the ER where she was safe, able to breathe through the breathing chamber, and under watchful eye yes of kind vet techs. The whole car ride to the ER I was holding Kiki tight in my arms. I would give anything in the world to have that moment again. To feel her heart beating against mine. I can never do that again. That whole day felt like running a marathon waiting for the next test result and then starting another one. Unfortunately the most important echocardiogram results came back late in the afternoon. There wasn't much more time for Kiki. The medical team only began the blood thinning medicine at 6 pm Hawaii time. Kiki was showing good signs of attention, and she still had her glow of good health. Then, all of a sudden right at 6:10 pm she dropped. All hands were on deck to give her CPR and they desperately tried to bring her back. But she was gone. The blood clot exploded causing a massive heart attack. I was weeping over her body for two hours. Her soul was already on its way to heaven. I couldn't accept that Kiki wasn't waking up. She looked so peaceful and wonderful like she was only napping. She died without any pain, yet the whole time I was under excruciating pain.

It was the most devastating experience, not only for me, but for thousands of people worldwide. Announcing "Princess Kiki has crossed the rainbow bridge..." on our Instagram page was the hardest thing I ever had to do. My my fingers were shaking as I typed out the post. Immediately within milliseconds of the post going live, a deluge of distress swept all across Instagram. Thousands of comments poured over my notifications feed and hundreds of direct messages crowded my inbox. "Everyone loves Kiki." was the first line of a comment that I read that totally tore me apart. Yes, everyone did love Kiki, and this first day of despair was the highest level of engagement on our page ever. From all ends of the planet, people were reposting Kiki's photos on their Instagram wall and stories. Digital memorials with music, photo collages, and artworks were designed with so much thoughtfulness. Hashtags were created so everyone could join in under a common location to pay their respects. I had tears streaming down my face as I read through each and every comment on my Kiki funeral post. I could not believe how long some comments were. People were genuinely grieving with me. I was not alone in this abyss of sadness. I got voice messages of people crying and saying, "Even though I never met her in person, I still felt like I knew her." I had an overwhelming relief of comfort from all the support people gave me those first few days. Besides the digital support, there were loads of physical cards, gifts, and flowers. People called in to the local high-end flower shops here in Hawaii to have the most exceptional flower arrangements delivered to my home. I thought I knew what true love is, until I saw true love personified through the beautiful things people went out of their way to create. I was sent three uniquely crafted crystal butterfly necklaces, a large paw print memory stone, an engraved bracelet, a Sherpa lined blanket with photos printed on it, helpful books, sweet stickers, and more. People made groups to pitch in on purchasing the most exquisite things. One group sent two large wooden boards with paintings of Kiki's photos, handmade from the Netherlands. Another group sent a specially designed wind chime that was in the tune of Amazing Grace, along with a beautiful Angel Kiki figurine that looked just like her. I was blown away by the lengths people took to express their sympathy for my loss. Even in heaven, Kiki is being so generous and good to me. She left me with so many everlasting friendships from all around the world. Aloha Kiki became a celebrity for the pet Instagram community because she and I created a brand that was built upon love, beauty, strength, kindness, compassion, and happiness. This book is filled with the exact captions and photos we posted that touched the hearts of so many worldwide.

The Aloha Kiki legacy will continue on, thanks to all of YOU! Thank you for believing in our mission of what it means to live your best life!

Princess Kiki Sunshine is up in heaven watching over us, sparkling the sky with marvelous sunrises and sunsets, and occasionally visiting as a butterfly.

We invite you to continue to follow us @alohakiki808 on Instagram and meet our new addition to the family. Her name is Kiki Hanalei. We had to keep the first name Kiki because it is such a sentimental name for us. Hanalei will be the second name to differentiate the two girls. Hanalei means crescent bay in Hawaiian, which is so fitting because the moon shines through darkness, guiding our path to a new horizon. Loosing a pet is a very dark time, but we must still search for the glimmer of hope and open ourselves to what the next chapter will be. I am proud to say that this next chapter with baby Kiki Hanalei is already off to such a great start. She is super smart and very affectionate, just like her angel sister. God brought us together for a reason and I trust in Him to help me heal my broken heart through raising another beautiful girl to be the next ambassador of Aloha.

Thank you for reading my book and for being my friends. I am super grateful to each and every one of you!

Lots of Love,
Sofia Kehaulani Selbe

About the Author

Born from the sweetest hibiscus nectar found in the most fragrant flower on the highest branch of the tallest vine touching the longest arm of sunshine, Sofia Kehaulani Selbe was designed to be a beacon of light for the world. Her heart flourishes with compassion and kindness. Her mind proliferates with theory and reasoning.

Coming from a background of architecture, earning a bachelor's degree in environmental design, and graduating with honors, Sofia Kehaulani Selbe has had the blessing of a technical and artistic way of thinking. Being awarded semifinalist of the worldwide Berkeley Prize Essay Competition to represent Hawaii, she molded her thoughts into the spirit of aloha being personified through distinguished Hawaiian buildings. Sofia Kehaulani Selbe has always enjoyed painting, drawing, sewing, cooking, and designing. She wants to use her talents as tools for inspiring others. Especially from her writing, Sofia Kehaulani Selbe can develop new ways to reach the deepest needs of our souls. This will be her first book, and she has poured her light into each page of it.

CPSIA information can be obtained
at www.ICGtesting.com
Printed in the USA
BVHW050926200421
605396BV00010B/2096

9 781098 034566